Magic Pony

Worst Week at School

"That's a rat trap all right," said Ned, skidding to a halt. "At the slightest touch the trap will spring."

They were just in time, for scrambling down the tunnel from the other direction came a beast so huge that Annie was suddenly terrified. The beast, which of course was Danny, twitched his whiskers at the sight of a girl on a pony and tested the air with his nose.

"Lance the cheese, Annie," shouted Ned, prancing forward, "before he comes any closer!"

**Join Annie on all her adventures
with Ned, the Magic Pony!**

Magic Pony

Worst Week at School

Elizabeth Lindsay
Illustrated by John Eastwood

A
LITTLE APPLE
PAPERBACK

SCHOLASTIC INC.

New York Toronto London Auckland Sydney
Mexico City New Delhi Hong Kong Buenos Aires

For Rupert

ISBN 0-439-44648-1
Text copyright © 1999 Elizabeth Lindsay.
Illustrations copyright © 1999 John Eastwood.

All rights reserved. Published by Scholastic, Inc., 557 Broadway, New York, NY 10012, by arrangement with Scholastic Children's Books, Scholastic Ltd. SCHOLASTIC, Little Apple, and associated logos are trademarks and/or registered trademarks of Scholastic Inc.

12 11 10 9 8 7 6 5 4 3 2   2 3 4 5 6 7/0

Printed in the U.S.A.
First Scholastic printing, October 2002

Chapter 1

The "Favorite Thing" Picture

Annie sat at the desk in her bedroom, felt-tip pen poised above a large sheet of white paper. She looked at the funny head she had drawn — two little ears, two black button eyes, a pointy nose, and lots of whiskers. The body had four pink feet and a long thin tail. She swung around to the pony poster on the wall above her chest of drawers.

"Ned, look what I've drawn," she said. "Danny, the rat!"

The pony in the poster looked out with pricked ears, his chestnut forelock tumbling over a white blaze, but he said nothing. His brown eyes stared over Annie's shoulder into a distance that was way beyond her bedroom wall. "Dear

Ned, I wish your magic would work. It hasn't in such a long time."

"Wish whose magic would work?" The voice came from the door, not the poster, as Annie so badly wanted, and it made her jump.

"Jamie, I wish you wouldn't do that!"

"Do what?"

"Creep up on me."

"If you didn't spend so much time talking to yourself then you'd hear me coming."

Her mouth opened to protest, but instead of saying she wasn't talking to herself, Annie said nothing. "Besides," Jamie continued, "if you want magic, then you only have to come to me. The Amazing Jamie Abracadabra Deakin — the most famous magician in the whole world."

"You wish," said Annie, grinning at her brother in spite of herself.

"By the time I'm grown up I will be. Mr. Cosby thinks I will. You wait and see."

"Well," said Annie, "if Mr. Cosby thinks you will . . . then maybe."

Jamie bought all his magic tricks from Mr. Cosby's shop — Cosby's Magic Emporium — and it was from there that Annie had bought the pony poster of Ned. It was a very special poster, too, because when it worked, Ned's magic was the most wonderful thing ever. It was also Annie's biggest secret.

"Do you want to see what I've drawn?"

Jamie groaned. "Not another horse picture."

Annie held up the drawing. "It's Danny, our class rat."

"That's a change from neverending ponies," said Jamie with surprise.

Annie glanced up at Ned's poster. So far Jamie hadn't realized there was anything special about the pony picture on her wall, and that was the way she was going to keep it.

"Oh," Jamie said, as if suddenly remembering. "Mom says you've got to hurry up, otherwise you'll miss the bus." And, message delivered, he strode from the room and bounded downstairs.

"*Phew*, Ned! That was a close call. When I talk to you I should remember to close my door."

Annie got her school backpack and slid the drawing of Danny carefully inside before crossing to the window. On the windowsill, Annie's three china ponies were in a line facing her bed, and, in the field outside, Penelope Potter's pony, Pebbles, was grazing in the early morning sun.

"All three of you will look outdoors today," she told the china ponies. "Much more fun. Esmerelda, you can look toward Winchway Wood. Prince can look at Pebbles, and Percy can look toward Pebbles's stable and be the first to see me when I come home from school. There! I

hope you have an interesting day and think up lots of daydreams for yourselves. I'd like to think up a daydream with Ned, but I haven't got time now."

Then, with a quick "good-bye" she picked up her backpack and raced from the room.

Annie didn't have time for a proper daydream on the school bus, either. She hurried to a free seat, eager to start one, while Jamie went to the back of the bus to join his friends. After saying hello, Penelope Potter sat down in front of her and saved a place for her best friend, Trudi. The daydream had gotten as far as Annie climbing onto Ned's back and her magic riding clothes appearing when the bus drew up at Trudi's stop.

By the time Ned had gone from being as large as Pebbles to becoming as small as china pony Percy, which he would if his magic were truly working, Trudi and Penelope were leaning over the backs of their seats. Although Annie wanted to keep on being a tiny person riding along the windowsill, it was impossible with two nosy faces peering around at her.

"Haven't you two got anything better to do than stare at me?" Annie asked.

"We're only being friendly," said Penelope.

Trudi's face stretched into one of her elastic smiles. "We want to see your picture."

Annie was instantly on guard, not wanting her drawing to get crumpled or torn.

"I'm not getting it out now," she said. "The bus is bumping all over the place. You'll have to wait until school."

Trudi's smile almost reached her ears. "Oh, come on, Annie. We know how good you are at drawing."

"Especially, 'specially good," chimed in Penelope.

"Yes, so pleeeease show us."

"No, show me yours first and I might," Annie said.

"Go on, Penelope." Trudi gave her friend a nudge.

"No," said Penelope. "You show yours first."

"You know I can't. I didn't do a very good one."

"Well I don't see why I should," complained Penelope.

Both girls slid down into their seats, bickering. Annie breathed a sigh of relief. Best not to give in to those two. You could never tell what might happen. She tried continuing with the daydream but couldn't concentrate, and it faded away. Instead she thought of what lay ahead once the bus arrived at school.

This week they were beginning a project on *What We Do In School*, in preparation for parents' day, and Mr. Beamish had asked them all to draw a picture of something they particularly liked about school. The best pictures would go in the display.

Annie had thought of drawing Danny sitting on their teacher's shoulder — which he loved to do when Mr. Beamish was writing on the blackboard — but in the end she didn't. She had filled her paper with a large picture of Danny by himself and was anxious to see it pinned up, knowing Mom and Dad would love it. She tucked her hand protectively around her backpack.

This was a smart move, because creeping fingers had taken hold of the strap and the backpack was almost pulled from her grasp. She wrenched it back again.

"Ouch! That hurt."

"What do you think you're doing, Trudi? Just leave my things alone."

"You could have broken my arm, Annie Deakin. Now I've got a bruise."

The bus pulled up outside the school gates and the door opened. Annie seized her chance to make a quick getaway.

"You were stealing my backpack," she cried, flinging the words over her shoulder. "But I didn't mean to hurt your arm!"

It was always the same with Trudi. If she didn't get her own way, she'd just take things. So before there could be any more unpleasantness, Annie jumped onto the sidewalk and hurried off in search of her best friend, Robyn.

Chapter 2

Teacher Shock

Robyn was waiting for Annie on the bench in their special place under the maple tree, her nose in a book as usual. As Annie approached she looked up, her welcoming grin fading when she saw the expression on Annie's face.

"What's up?" she asked, shoving the book in her schoolbag.

"It's Trudi, as usual. She tried stealing my backpack to sneak a look at my picture. She says I bruised her arm. But I didn't mean to."

"Typical! At least she didn't get it." Robyn patted the bench beside her and Annie sat down. "Did you draw Danny like you said?" Annie carefully took out her picture. "It's perfect," said Robyn. "Just like him. I can almost see his whiskers twitching. I bet that it gets in the display."

"With luck," said Annie. "What did you do?"

Robyn was passionate about reading, so Annie expected a picture with books in it, but when she looked at what Robyn had drawn, it was so different from what she'd imagined, she burst out laughing.

There was a classroom with a book teacher and book pupils, each with little arms and legs sticking out from their book bodies. Underneath the story titles on the covers, Robyn had painted smiling faces, and all the book people held tiny reading books.

"Awesome, Rob. Mr. Beamish'll love that."

"I hope so. There's a book person for each of us in the class, and it took forever to draw. I printed all my favorite titles on the covers."

The bell rang and they tucked their pictures back into their bags and hurried into school. They were on their way into the classroom when they bumped into Penelope and Trudi.

"Your arm OK?" Annie asked.

"No thanks to you," said Trudi with a frown, and shoved her way in front to burst in first through the classroom door — which, it turned out, was a mistake.

Waiting by the teacher's table was a tall, stern-looking lady with wispy gray hair pulled back in a bun. She looked down at Trudi and wrinkled her nose as if the girl was something smelly. Next to this forbidding lady stood Mrs. Smedley, the principal. Entering the classroom, the pupils fell silent one by one, each turning to shush the others behind.

The class stared at the stranger with wide eyes as they filed to their places. Where was Mr. Beamish? The stranger stared back, her quick eyes darting from one pupil to the next. This was no longer an ordinary morning, and while the class waited for their principal's explanation, Annie had the awful feeling that something horrible was about to happen. Mrs. Smedley cleared her throat.

"Good morning, class."

"Good morning, Mrs. Smedley."

"I'd like to introduce you to Miss Pike, who has kindly come in to teach you while Mr. Beamish is away this week." There was a muted groan. Miss Pike's beady eyes glinted and her long neck seemed to sway. A hush fell at once. "Now, I'm sure you'll make Miss Pike feel at home, class, and that you'll have an enjoyable week."

"Thank you, Mrs. Smedley," said Miss Pike, smiling politely while waiting for the principal to leave. The moment the classroom door closed, Miss Pike said, "Sit." The class sat. "Not like that. Not like that. No scraping of chairs. Lift them. Lift them."

Everyone sat as quietly as possible and tried not to move a muscle. Annie turned briefly to Robyn and made an *isn't this terrible* face. A flicker of panic signaled in Robyn's eyes, but she was too late.

"You, girl. Yes, you. Stand up."

Annie swallowed. Miss Pike was pointing at her. Slowly she stood up.

"Name?"

"Annie."

"Annie? Annie what? Full name. Out with it."

"Annie Deakin."

"Very well. Annie Deakin. Let it be understood that from this moment we have no making faces in this room by you or any other member of this class. Remain standing. You — now you stand up." This time the finger was pointing at Trudi. "You. The girl who pushed her way so rudely into class. Up. Up. Name?"

"Trudi Tyler."

"Trudi Tyler. And pray tell, Trudi Tyler, what required such an ill-mannered entry into the peaceful domain of this pleasant classroom?" Trudi stepped backward into her chair, making it scrape, and Miss Pike's eyes bulged from their sockets.

"I . . . I . . . I . . ." stuttered Trudi.

"Out with it, child!" But Trudi was so frightened by Miss Pike's wild stare that she could not manage another word.

"It was my fault," said Annie, jumping in to save the situation.

"Your fault?" Miss Pike's beady gaze landed on Annie and she folded her arms. "Then explain, Annie Deakin. I am waiting."

Annie took a deep breath. "On the school bus Trudi's arm somehow got hurt, which made her angry and she came into class a little fast."

"Are you trying to tell me you deliberately harmed Trudi?"

"No, no, not deliberately. Trudi wanted to see the picture I'd drawn for Mr. Beamish and I didn't want to show it. Her arm got hurt by mistake."

"A picture for Mr. Beamish? Bring it to me at once."

Reluctantly, Annie pulled out the drawing of Danny. Miss Pike held out her hand. "I will not have squabbling in my class, Annie Deakin, as you will find out."

Annie walked slowly to the front of the class and offered up the picture. Miss

Pike shook the paper and peered at the drawing. Then she gave Annie one of her wrinkled-nose looks and turned the paper the other way up — as if it was Annie's fault she was looking at the picture upside down.

But when she looked at it the right-way up her nose wrinkled even more and she held out the paper at arm's length, as if it was something quite disgusting.

Trying not to move a muscle, Annie held her breath, and so, it seemed, did everyone else in the class. Then, through the silence, came the *scrabble*, *scrabble* sound of tiny feet rustling in paper.

"Who's making that noise?" demanded Miss Pike.

"It's Danny," said Annie.

"Stand up, Daniel, at once!"

"No, no, look," said Annie, and ran to the back of the classroom, where she lifted the lid from a glass cage and rummaged in a nest of shredded paper. "This is who my picture's of." And she proudly carried Danny to the front of the room. "He's our class's brown rat and it's my turn to look after him this week."

Danny, who had just awakened from a satisfying sleep, twitched his nose, wiggled his whiskers, and looked Miss Pike straight in the eye.

Miss Pike turned to stone, or so it appeared, and her glasses slid down her nose. There was a moment of terrible silence. Then, totally unexpectedly, she jumped onto the teacher's chair. "Vermin!" she cried, waving both of them away with Annie's picture. "Filthy vermin. Put it back in its cage at once."

Annie hurried to obey, clutching the startled Danny, who wriggled to escape.

She managed to get him back into the cage, where he squeezed from her clutches and burrowed into the safety of his nest. Annie quickly put back the lid and turned her own pale face toward the new teacher, aware that Miss Pike's squinting eyes followed her every move.

"Do not remove that creature from its cage again. Do you understand?"

"Yes. Miss Pike."

The teacher stepped down from the chair, fanning herself with the picture. "In my opinion, the only good rat is a dead . . ." She caught sight of the sea of shocked faces and didn't finish. "Gracious me, we must get going. Time and tide wait for no one." Then with a little shiver, she ripped Annie's picture into tiny pieces and dropped the bits into the wastepaper basket. The class was stunned. Annie had the dreadful feeling that if Miss Pike wasn't so scared of Danny, she would have ripped him to pieces as well. "Sit, Trudi Tyler." Trudi crumpled into her place.

There was a deathly hush while the class waited for whatever was coming next.

"Annie Deakin, go and wash your hands and use plenty of soap. Get rid of all those disgusting rat germs."

Miss Pike tapped her bun to make sure it was still in place before curling her lips into a smile. But everyone could see her eyes were as piercing as ever. "Now,

class, take out your English books. You are going to show me how well you can write."

Annie slunk to the sink at the back of the classroom and turned on the tap. She could hardly believe that her wonderful picture lay shredded at the bottom of the wastepaper basket. And worse, poor Danny must be as frightened as she was, and there was nothing she could do to comfort him.

Chapter 3

Rat Escape

At recess the class gathered outside in the playground in unusually subdued and whispering groups. They took this opportunity to say how sorry they were that Annie's picture was torn up — even Trudi, who looked horribly pale and kept leaning on Penelope as if she was going to faint.

"It's when she looks at you," Trudi groaned. "Her eyes bore right into you."

"She must be the worst teacher in the world to tear up such a good drawing," said Robyn. "I saw the picture and it was great."

"She's horrible," muttered Penelope. "Mr. Beamish had better come back soon, that's all I can say."

It was Annie who was most worried. "The worst thing is she hates rats, and Danny's all on his own in the classroom with no one to protect him."

"But what can she do to him?" asked Robyn. "He's our class pet."

"Poison him," said Penelope. "I bet she's the sort of person who carries rat poison around in her handbag."

"She wouldn't," said Annie. "Would she?"

Yet when everyone filed back into class after playtime, they found Miss Pike patrolling up and down the classroom, smacking a ruler on tabletops in between ducking to look at the floor. Annie and Robyn noticed at once that the lid was

halfway off Danny's cage and exchanged anxious glances.

"Sit," said Miss Pike.

Carefully lifting their chairs, the class sat.

"Own up," said Miss Pike, turning on them at once. "Which of you has removed the rat from its cage?"

Her accusation was met by shocked murmurs and wide-eyed, disbelieving faces. Annie put up her hand.

"So it was you, Annie Deakin? I might have guessed."

"No, no. I just wanted to say that Danny might have pushed the lid off."

"And why would that be? Because the girl who put him back in his cage didn't put the lid back on properly?"

"No, I did put the lid back on properly. It's just that usually by now Danny's had lots of exercise in his rat run."

"His rat run?" Miss Pike huffed. "What's that?"

Annie pointed to the back of the classroom. Miss Pike turned to stare at a series of brightly painted cardboard tubes and boxes, decorated with flowers, birds, and butterflies, that ran along the rear wall and under the window.

"The boxes and tubes are his rat run. They're all connected. Mr. Beamish lets Danny run up and down inside it all day if he wants to. He could be in it now for all we know."

Miss Pike scuttled to the front of the class and stood on her chair brandishing her ruler. "Search the room, class! Pick up those boxes and shake the rodent out. It must be found."

"But if we shake the rat run it might break," said Annie.

"I don't care."

No one moved a muscle until Miss Pike smashed her ruler down on the table and shrieked, "GET A MOVE ON!"

Suddenly, everyone in the class was scuttling here and there, looking up tubes and shaking boxes, crawling under tables and looking behind books on bookshelves. Annie carefully checked Danny's nest to make sure it was empty, then got down beside Robyn under a table.

"I'm sure I put the lid back on properly," she whispered.

Robyn glanced over her shoulder. "Miss Pike could be making it up about Danny's escape. She could have done what Penelope said and poisoned him."

"Oh, this is terrible." Annie groaned. "What will we tell Mr. Beamish when he comes back? He really loves Danny."

After all the searching, the rat run had come apart in the middle, and it was a very sad class who finally had to admit defeat and say they couldn't find their special pet.

"Very well," said Miss Pike. "Sit, class. Lessons must go on in spite of this outrage. Take out your math books. We are here to work, class, not to waste time. And wasting time is what we have been doing." Looking warily at the floor, Miss Pike stepped down from her chair. "A rat is a rat. For the present let it roam. It won't bother me."

Annie took out her math book and thought that if Miss Pike expected them to believe that, she was not very good at pretending. The teacher's gaze kept darting to the floor and she had a tight hold on the ruler.

"I don't think she has poisoned him," Annie whispered. "She's too frightened."

"Let's hope you're right," whispered back Robyn.

Hours later, after lots of hard work, there was still no sign of Danny, and Annie had writer's cramp. She had done all the math problems and was certain she had the right answers. It was Robyn who was struggling miserably. Annie leaned across the table, wishing she could help. Mr. Beamish always let her when Robyn was stuck.

"Annie Deakin, what are you doing?"

Miss Pike advanced toward her, tapping the ruler into her palm.

"I think Robyn needs some help," said Annie.

"If Robyn cannot do the work by herself then she must put up her hand. Do you need help, Robyn?"

"Yes. No. Well, sort of."

"Either you do or you don't. Speak up, girl."

"Yes," said Robyn. "I'm stuck. It's really difficult." And under Miss Pike's stern gaze she burst into tears.

"Oh, for goodness sake, stop that unnecessary sniveling and sit up," snapped Miss Pike.

Annie pulled a tissue from her pocket and passed it to her fried. "I don't think it's fair to make Robyn cry when she's trying her hardest. No one ever cries when Mr. Beamish is here." There was an eerie silence while Miss Pike turned her stony gaze on Annie.

"Annie Deakin," said the oily voice, "if you dare speak to me like that again, you will be severely punished. I can think of several ways to make your life extremely unpleasant." Miss Pike brought her face down until Annie became almost cross-eyed looking at the point of her nose. "Do you understand, Annie?"

Annie didn't dare move a muscle. "Yes, Miss Pike."

"You are a troublemaker and I do not like troublemakers. The sooner you mend your ways, the better." The bell rang. "And just to show you that I mean what I say, you can spend your lunchtime in here looking for that rat." Miss Pike glanced nervously at the floor. "Do I make myself clear, Annie?"

"Yes, Miss Pike."

"Books away, class. You are dismissed."

When everyone but Annie had filed from the classroom, Miss Pike hurried to go, too. She turned back in time to say, "Don't just sit there, Annie. Start looking!" before slamming the door.

"Danny, Danny, where are you?" called Annie as she began another hopeless search. Eventually, she took out her lunch box and scattered pieces of tomato sandwich at one end of the rat run, hoping to tempt Danny out — although deep down she knew he wasn't in there. She ate the rest before deciding to look one more time. She was on her hands and knees peering down a cardboard tube when Mrs. Smedley found her.

"Oh, Annie, dear, have you found him?"

"No," cried Annie. "It's terrible! Miss Pike hates rats, and what'll Mr. Beamish say?"

"Don't worry, Danny will turn up. He can't have gone far. You go and join your friends in the playground and I'll have a look."

"Miss Pike says I have to stay here," said Annie.

"I'll tell Miss Pike I gave you permission, and if I find Danny I'll take him to my office."

Later, when they came back to class, it was obvious Mrs. Smedley hadn't found Danny. His cage was still empty at the back of the classroom. Miss Pike placed her chair on top of the teacher's desk and, clutching her ruler, sat at this great height for the rest of the afternoon, glaring down at the class and issuing orders.

When the bell rang she quickly dismissed everybody, jumped down to the floor, and hurried from the classroom. Annie hung back. After all, it was her turn to clean his cage and feed Danny this week and she wanted to have one last look.

"You'll miss your bus," said Robyn.

"Danny's in here somewhere. I just want to find him."

"He's done the most sensible thing," said Robyn. "He's found somewhere really safe and out of Miss Pike's way. If he's smart, he'll stay there till Mr. Beamish gets back next week."

"But if we find him we could take him to Mrs. Smedley's office. He'd be safe there."

"We haven't got time," said Robyn. "If we don't hurry we'll both miss our buses." And she took hold of Annie's arm and pulled her from the classroom.

Chapter 4

Ned Comes to School

It wasn't until after dinner that Annie was finally able to shut her bedroom door, sit on the bed next to the furry, fast-asleep bundle that was Tabitha, her cat, and have a proper talk with the pony in the poster on her wall. She poured out the disastrous story of how Mr. Beamish was not in school this week and how, instead, the class had Miss Pike, a teacher so horrible that she had torn up her drawing of Danny.

"But the most awful of all is that Danny has escaped," Annie groaned. "Miss Pike hates rats. If she finds him before we do, she might do something terrible."

She gazed up at the pony in the poster, and although he was still a smooth, shiny, picture pony, he looked as if he had heard every word.

There was a knock and Dad popped his head in the door.

"It's time you were putting on your pajamas," he said. "It's getting late. I'll be back in ten minutes to say good night."

When she lay tucked in bed with Tabitha curled on her feet, Annie closed her eyes and wished her hardest.

"Please, Ned, let your magic work tomorrow," she begged. "You haven't been out of your poster for such a long time and you'd know what to do about Miss Pike." Then with a little sigh, she turned over and, trying not to think of the horrible new teacher, closed her eyes.

It took forever to get to sleep, and when she did, she tossed and turned, tumbling into a dark dream in which she found herself in a room stacked high with giant sacks labeled RAT POISON. Annie knew at once she was in a cellar under the school. Footsteps echoed around her and she tried to hide but found she couldn't move. A tall figure towered over her and turned into Miss Pike. Annie was scared. From beneath a flowing cloak, the teacher took out a small glass cage. She thought the cage was empty but Miss Pike's triumphant smile made Annie look again. Inside was Danny, the rat.

"Annie," called Danny, scrabbling at the sides. "Help me!"

Annie tried to snatch him but Miss Pike laughed and held the cage out of reach.

"You, Annie, you are going to feed this vile rodent the poison."

"No!" Annie cried. "No, I won't!"

"Annie!" called the rat again, and this time when she stretched out her hand to grab him, she floated away from the dark cellar and Danny was left behind. Another voice whispered her name, but so softly that at first she didn't hear it.

"Danny!" She sobbed. "Danny, where are you?"

"Annie, wake up. It's me, Ned. You've had a bad dream."

Gentle pony lips brushed away the tears on her cheeks. Annie rolled over and opened her eyes. There beside the bed, filling up all the space between the door and the wall, was her magic pony.

"Ned!" she cried. "Oh, Ned, you've come out of your poster at last." And she flung her arms about his neck and buried her face in his chestnut mane.

"There, there," said Ned. "It was only a dream." And he nuzzled her close. "Tell me all about it."

"It was Miss Pike, in a cellar under the school, and she was going to poison Danny. We've got to find him before she does. We've got to, Ned."

"And we will," said Ned. "But first you must get up."

Tabitha was still fast asleep, but the sun peeping in through the crack in the curtains announced it was morning. Annie felt much better now that Ned had come out of his poster, even though the moment she put her feet on the carpet the magic wind blew and he was gone. She knew he wouldn't be far away and dropped down on her hands and knees to look. There, in front of her, galloped a tiny chestnut pony, his mane and tail flying wildly just as if he were the china Percy come to life. Ned twisted and turned, took a flying leap over one of Annie's sneakers, and came to a prancing stop in front of her.

"Hurry up," he said. "We're going to get to school early."

"But what about the bus?"

"You don't need the bus when you can ride me!"

"Ned!" Annie's eyes shone. "I'll be ready in two seconds, but I'll have to have breakfast, otherwise Mom'll wonder what's going on."

"Of course," said Ned. "I'll wait in your backpack." He trotted across the carpet and jumped into the front pocket. "Now hurry up. Oh, and bring a flashlight. We may need it."

Annie didn't need telling twice. She added her pocket flashlight to the things in her backpack and was washed, dressed, and downstairs in no time, surprising Mom with her early start. She ate some toast, picked up her lunch box and grabbed her backpack.

"See you later, Mom," she called and was gone.

Annie was hurrying past Penelope's stable yard when Ned said, "In here." The yard was empty, and as soon as they were out of sight behind the hedge, Ned jumped from the backpack, landing proper pony size beside her, wearing his saddle and bridle, ready for her to mount.

Annie took hold of the reins and sprang onto his back. As soon as she was in the saddle her school clothes vanished and she was dressed in a velvet hard hat, riding jacket, jodhpurs, and jodhpur boots, while her backpack was transformed into a pair of saddlebags which hung across Ned's back. Wearing the magic riding clothes was her perfect disguise. No one would recognize her as Annie Deakin now. Annie adjusted her chin strap and was ready to go.

"Hold tight!" cried Ned.

Annie expected him to turn onto the road, but instead he cantered toward the field, leaping the gate before galloping by the surprised Pebbles, who just a moment before had been quietly grazing. The dappled gray pony kicked up his heels and galloped alongside until Ned leaped over the far hedge, leaving Pebbles to watch them go.

"Ned, where are we going?" Annie cried.

"Straight across country to school. It's the quickest way for a horse."

The speed was thrilling. Annie stood in her stirrups and counted strides at each hedge and ditch they jumped, while the wind whistled and her eyes watered. *What a way to come to school*, she thought, and wished she could ride there like this every day.

Before she realized it, Ned was galloping across the deserted playing field. It looked as though they were early enough to have the school to themselves.

"We'll take a look in your classroom window," said Ned, "and then we'll decide what to do."

Annie lay low on Ned's neck while he crept beside the wall.

"Look," she said, noticing that one of the windows wasn't properly shut. "If I pulled that open we could get in there."

Annie stood in her stirrups and leaned along Ned's neck and together they peered into the classroom to make sure it was empty. Only it wasn't.

"It's Miss Pike!" Annie gasped.

"So that's her, is it?" whispered Ned. "She's up to something."

Miss Pike was wearing pink rubber

gloves and holding some kind of gadget. As they watched, she stuck what looked like a chunk of yellow cheese on the gadget before placing it in the broken part of Danny's rat run.

"It's a trap," said Ned.

"A rat trap?" Annie was horrified. "I knew she'd do something like this."

Next, Miss Pike pulled out a roll of tape and spent several minutes taping up the cardboard. At last, she appeared satisfied and pulled off the pink gloves. She stuffed both gloves and the tape in her handbag, then, with a quick look over her shoulder, hurried from the classroom.

"We must be quick," said Ned.
"Danny'll smell the cheese in no time.
For a hungry rat a piece that size is a feast.
We must get there before he does."

"Let's go!" cried Annie and, leaning
over, pulled the window open. Ned turned
in a circle and galloped toward the
opening. He took a mighty leap into a
blast of magic wind while Annie clung
on and closed her eyes.

Chapter 5

Rat Trap

They landed inside on the windowsill, a tiny pony and tiny rider in what seemed like a giant's classroom. Annie was amazed at the hugeness of it, but Ned wasted no time and jumped to the top of the bookshelf.

"What we need is a pencil," he cried.

"I've got one in my pencil case," said Annie.

"Good thinking," said Ned, skidding to a stop while Annie unbuckled one of the saddlebags. She found her pencil case and took out a pencil.

"It won't be any good at that tiny size," said Ned, as Annie rebuckled the saddlebag. He maneuvered himself next to a pile of books. "Put the pencil on top here and let go."

Annie did as she was told and quick as a wink the miniature pencil became its real size, which seemed gigantic to her.

"What's it for?" she asked.

"It's to make a lance. Can you pick it up?"

Annie wrapped her arm around the pencil and lifted it.

"Just about."

"Good. You're going to spring the rat trap with it."

Ned trotted to the end of the bookcase, and Annie leaned back, holding on tightly to the pencil, as Ned dropped to the table below. They hit the shiny top and began to slide. The edge came closer and closer and, realizing they weren't going to stop, Annie swung the pencil eraser onto the table top and used it as a brake.

"Good job!" cried Ned, steadying his feet at last before jumping onto a chair and taking a final leap to the floor.

Annie breathed a sigh of relief and tucked the pencil back under her arm while Ned set off at a gallop, racing between the table and chair legs to the place in the rat run where Miss Pike had set the trap. They arrived, panting, to find that the tape completely covered the hole and they couldn't get in — not even when Annie prodded the tape with the pencil point.

Wasting no time, Ned turned on his haunches and galloped for the nearest rat run entrance, racing past a jungle of flowers and butterflies spreading high above them, before trotting into the dark. Once they were inside, Annie let go of the reins and fumbled in one of the saddlebags for her flashlight.

"Listen," said Ned. "I can hear something."

Echoing down the tube came a distant pitter-patter of clawed feet.

"It's Danny!" whispered Annie. "He must have come in at the other end."

"Yes," agreed Ned. "And he's heading straight for the cheese."

They had no time to lose. Holding the pencil tightly with one hand, Annie shone the flashlight with the other, leaving the steering to Ned. With reins flying, the pony raced down the cardboard tunnel, galloping into a cavern of a box.

"Now where?" he asked, champing at the bit.

There were three tubes running off the far side of the box, but Annie was sure the top two tubes doubled back on themselves.

"Down there," she said, pointing the flashlight, hoping she was right. This tube twisted and turned. The class had made it that way on purpose so it would be more fun for Danny — but it slowed his rescuers down.

"If I'm remembering it right, the break's through one more box and into the next tube," said Annie.

Ned raced across the floor of the next large box and, guided by the flashlight beam, sped into the opposite tube.

"There it is," cried Annie as the flashlight lit up an innocent-looking yellow lump the size of a hefty rock that lay in their path.

"That's a rat trap all right," said Ned, skidding to a halt. "At the slightest touch the trap will spring."

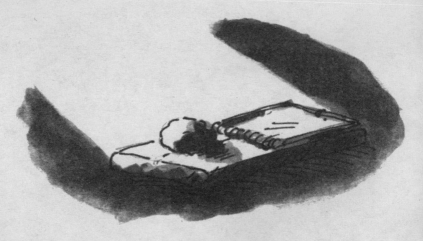

They were just in time, for scrambling down the tunnel from the other direction came a beast so huge that Annie was suddenly terrified. The beast, which of course was Danny, twitched his whiskers at the sight of a girl on a pony and tested the air with his nose.

"Lance the cheese, Annie," shouted Ned, prancing forward, "before he comes any closer!" Annie took aim. She thrust the pencil into the cheese and let go. The trap snapped, splintering the pencil into pieces. Stunned by the noise, none of them moved until Annie swung around in the saddle.

"Danny, it's nothing to worry about," she called, hoping he would recognize her voice.

The rat blinked twice and, unable to resist the cheese, reached out with his front paws and pulled it from its spike. Transferring it to his mouth, he pattered off with his prize.

Annie shone the flashlight over the remains of the pencil. "That could have been Danny," she said.

"Indeed," replied Ned. "All thanks to Miss Pike. We must go after him and find out where he's hiding."

Stepping around the trap, Ned set off in pursuit, following the pitter-patter of Danny's feet, catching the occasional glimpse of his tail in the flashlight beam. At last, they came out into a large box just in time to see Danny disappear through a jagged hole in the cardboard.

"This isn't the end of the run," said Annie. "Danny must have chewed a way out."

They slipped through the hole, following Danny behind Mr. Beamish's bookcase. Here they discovered another rat-sized entrance.

"This must be his secret hiding place," said Annie.

Danny didn't try to stop them from coming in, but sat back on his haunches, nibbling hungrily, keeping a watchful eye on them as if to say, "This cheese is all mine."

Annie's heart was pounding. Being as tiny as they were made Danny seem enormous, more like a hairy monster than the friendly brown rat she knew.

"Don't be frightened, Annie. He knows who you are," said Ned. "And he's the same old Danny."

"Yes," said Annie. "Of course he is." She put out a hand to stroke his fur. "Oh, Danny, I'm so glad we've found you. When you've finished your breakfast, we'll think of what to do next."

The school bell rang, which made Annie jump.

"There's no need to worry," said Ned, lifting his nose to look over a pile of books. "We're very safe in this cupboard and we can stay hidden here all day if we have to."

Annie relaxed, watching the lump of cheese grow smaller, until she heard the sharp tones of Miss Pike's voice. It sent a chill right through her.

"Come in, class, and stand at your chairs."

There was a swish of footsteps and a rustle of schoolbags being put on the floor, then silence. "Sit — and do it quietly." There was none of the expectant murmuring heard when Mr. Beamish was their teacher.

"And pray tell, where is that trouble-maker Annie Deakin this morning?" The class remained silent. "Hands up."

"Please, Miss Pike?"

"WAIT UNTIL YOU ARE SPOKEN TO, PENELOPE." There was another pause, then Miss Pike's pretending-to-be-nice voice. "Yes, Penelope?"

"Annie wasn't on the school bus this morning, Miss Pike."

"So she missed the bus, did she? It doesn't surprise me. But no doubt we shall have a more peaceful day without her. Take out your math books, class. Robyn, your work was a disgrace. If there's no improvement this morning you will stay in at recess and lunchtime and do them all again. Do you understand?"

"Yes, Miss Pike."

At the sound of Robyn's hurt voice, Annie grew hot with rage. "It's not Robyn's fault. She tries really hard," Annie whispered. "Miss Pike is the worst."

"Yes," said Ned. "She certainly is."

With the cheese gone, Danny licked his paws and washed his whiskers. From the silence of the classroom came the familiar tap and scrape of chalk on the blackboard. The rat pricked up his ears. Then, without warning, he brushed past them and jumped from the back of the cupboard.

"Oh, Ned! When Mr. Beamish writes on the blackboard Danny likes to sit on his shoulder."

"Well, if he sits on Miss Pike's shoulder, it might be just the thing to frighten her away."

Ned squeezed between some books and they both peered out through a crack in the bookcase to see Miss Pike busy writing up math problems and Danny scuttling purposefully across the classroom floor toward her.

Chapter 6

Teacher Scare

The chalk squeak-squeaked on the blackboard.

"Write down these problems in your best handwriting, class. You have ten minutes to do them." Miss Pike wrote up more and more problems and the chalk kept squeaking.

"It's not fair," said Annie. "Robyn'll

never do all those problems in ten minutes."

Danny reached the teacher's table. He jumped for the chair and hauled himself up.

"Ned, I've got to get out of this bookcase before something terrible happens."

"Agreed," said Ned.

With a huge leap, Danny flew through the air and landed halfway up the back of Miss Pike's woolen dress, where he clung on with his claws. Miss Pike swung around to face the class.

"WHO THREW THAT?" she roared. Most of the class had seen Danny and there was a shocked and deathly hush. When he climbed up on Miss Pike's shoulder, the teacher slowly turned her head and came eyeball-to-eyeball with him. She let out a loud scream, and Danny, realizing his mistake, jumped for the table.

"Vermin!" Miss Pike shrieked. "Kill it! Kill it!"

She hit out with her ruler. *Thwack! Thwack!* Danny dodged, and on the third *thwack!* the ruler snapped. He leaped from the table and raced across the floor. Seeing him go, Miss Pike grasped the nearest thing, her handbag, and threw it at him.

The attack was too much for the class. "Leave Danny alone!" they cried, and

soon Miss Pike was being pelted with pens and math books, pencil cases and erasers.

"Now's your chance, Annie," said Ned. The pony swung around, jumped through the hole in the back of the cupboard, and galloped behind the rat run. "You can get off now. Leave the backpack here for me to hide in," he cried.

"How dare you side with a rodent!" Miss Pike screamed above the uproar. "How dare you throw things at me!"

Annie quickly dismounted but kept hold of the reins. The corner space she was in seemed huge, but she realized it was best to crouch down on her hands and knees before letting go. The magic wind blew and she found herself squashed between the wall and the rat run, back in her school clothes, with just enough room to pull off her backpack. She propped it up for the tiny Ned and he jumped into the front pocket.

"Danny's safe," he called. "He's gone back into the bookcase."

What a relief! But for Annie there was no going back. Although safely out of sight behind the rat run, she knew what she was going to do. Keeping on her hands and knees, she scuttled from behind the

run and under her table. Slowly the uproar faded. Annie knew why when she heard Mrs. Smedley's stern voice say, "Class, take your seats at once."

The moment Robyn sat down Annie tapped her on the knee. Annie knew she'd be surprised, but to Robyn's credit she didn't utter a sound. Instead, she watched as Annie made a cutting signal and, without drawing attention to herself, pulled her pointy scissors from her bag and handed them over.

"Perhaps you would explain to me what is going on, Miss Pike?" Mrs. Smedley asked.

"They set the rat on me," said Miss Pike, huffing and puffing. "I have never known such an unruly, ill-disciplined class. It climbed up my back. I could have had heart failure. Naturally, I screamed — as you do when you find a rat on your shoulder. Then they threw things at me."

"I see," said Mrs. Smedley. Annie scuttled to the back of the classroom. Several of the others had seen her by now, but she put a finger to her lips and, although surprised, no one said anything.

Annie reached the taped-up place in the rat run and pushed the scissors in. It was easy now, at her normal size, and soon she had cut open the hole. She felt inside.

"It's a conspiracy," said Miss Pike. "This class should be severely punished, every last one of them."

Annie wrapped her fingers around the trap and finally stood up.

"Please, Mrs. Smedley. Miss Pike set this in Danny's run." And she held up the rat trap for everyone to see.

"Annie Deakin!" screeched Miss Pike, her eyes popping with shocked surprise. "Where did you spring from?"

"And she wore pink rubber gloves when she was doing it," said Annie. "And stuck the rat run up with tape. But I sprang it with a pencil so it wouldn't work. The rubber gloves are in her handbag."

Miss Pike looked around quickly for her bag. It lay open on the floor where she had thrown it. Strewn in front of it, where they had fallen, were two pink rubber gloves.

"I see," said Mrs. Smedley. "Does anyone know where Danny is?"

"I do," said Annie. "I found his hiding place this morning." She longed to add "with help from my friend Ned," but didn't. "I came to school early. That's when I saw Miss Pike set the trap."

There was an astonished gasp from the class and Miss Pike's eyes narrowed dangerously. Annie was glad Mrs. Smedley was there. "That girl tells lies. Don't believe a word of it, Mrs. Smedley. She's a nasty, spying little toad."

Mrs. Smedley looked at Annie's earnest face and turned to the teacher by her side.

"Come to my office, please, Miss Pike," she said. "And Annie, find Danny and put him back in his cage. The rest of you sit quietly until I come back."

With a toss of her head, Miss Pike picked up her bag and the pink rubber gloves and marched from the classroom. Mrs. Smedley followed.

After that, sitting quietly was impossible.

"Did you spy on her?" Trudi asked. "I wish I'd thought of that."

"I wish I'd thought of getting to school early," said Penelope.

"Look, let Annie get Danny before you ask any questions," said Robyn.

Annie grinned. "Let's be really quiet so we don't frighten him," she said, and opened Mr. Beamish's bookcase. Taking out the books at the front, she found Danny crouched in a corner at the back. He seemed relieved to see her, and she picked him up and held him close.

"Poor Danny. You've had quite an adventure." Annie cuddled him all the way to his cage and gently put him inside. He gave a quick twitch of his whiskers before scampering to his nest and burrowing out of sight. Annie put the lid on and, to make sure it wouldn't come off again, placed three large books on top of it.

After that she found herself bombarded with questions, so, without mentioning Ned, she explained everything as best she could. It was a relief when Mrs. Smedley came back into the classroom.

"Sit down, everyone, and listen." The class scooted to their places. "Miss Pike will not be coming back . . ." There was a gasp of delight. Mrs. Smedley held up her hand for quiet. ". . . and I've just received a very special phone call from Mr.

Beamish. It's good news. Last night, his wife had a baby daughter — Alice Louise. He's bringing a photograph to show you next week." A burst of applause and a huge cheer followed this announcement. "In the meantime, you'll have to make do with me as your teacher."

Annie grinned with relief and Robyn grinned back. No more Miss Pike. Things were looking up. Robyn held up her hand.

"Please, Mrs. Smedley, can everyone sign my book picture so we can send it to say 'happy birthday' to Alice Louise from our class?"

"I think that's a lovely idea," said Mrs. Smedley. "Let's do it right away."

Annie got out her backpack. Checking in the front pocket, she glimpsed a chestnut mane and tail. Her magic pony was safe. Now there was nothing left to do but enjoy school again and, yes, draw a new picture of Danny. She took out her pencil case.

At the end of the day, when the school bus arrived at their stop, Annie said good-bye to Penelope. Then, to avoid any more of Jamie's nosy questions about why she hadn't been on the morning bus, she ran all the way home. Once indoors, she said a quick "hi" to her mom and rushed upstairs. Then, after closing her bedroom door, she put her backpack on the floor. With a leap, the tiny chestnut Ned landed on the carpet.

"I don't think Jamie believed me when I said I rode to school."

"He certainly didn't when you said it was on a horse." Ned laughed.

Outside, there were footsteps on the landing. The door burst open. In the blink of an eye, the pony was gone.

"OK, Jamie, now what do you want?" asked Annie.

"Mom just told me you left early enough to walk," said Jamie smugly. "So now I know riding to school was just one of your little daydreams."

"So everything's all right then," said Annie.

"And Mom also says she's astonished you didn't notice the chocolate cake she made for dessert, and are you coming to help eat it?"

"Yes," said Annie, looking wistfully at Ned — a pony picture once more. Jamie looked at him, too.

"You're always talking to that pony poster. That's probably why you make up such silly stories."

"Maybe I do and maybe I don't," said Annie with a secret smile. And giving Ned a cheerful wave, she set off downstairs for dinner.